D0266884

RABBIT & BEAR

A Bite in the Night

STORY BY
JULIAN GOUGH

ILLUSTRATIONS BY
JIM FIELD

Text copyright © Julian Gough 2019
Illustrations copyright © Jim Field 2019

First published in Great Britain in 2019
by Hodder Children's Books

The rights of Julian Gough and Jim Field to be identified as the Author and Illustrator
of the Work have been asserted by them in accordance with the Copyright, Designs
and Patents Act 1988.

1

All rights reserved. Apart from any use permitted under UK copyright law, this
publication may only be reproduced, stored or transmitted, in any form, or by
any means with prior permission in writing from the publishers or in the case of
reprographic production in accordance with the terms of licences issued by the
Copyright Licensing Agency and may not be otherwise circulated in any form
of binding or cover other than that in which it is published and without a similar
condition being imposed on the subsequent purchaser.

All characters in this publication are fictitious and any resemblance
to real persons, living or dead, is purely coincidental.

A Catalogue record for this book is available
from the British Library

ISBN 978 1 444 92174 8

Printed and bound in China by RRD

The paper and board used in this book are made from wood from responsible
sources.

Hodder Children's Books
A division of Hachette Children's Group
Carmelite House
50 Victoria Embankment
London EC4Y 0DZ

An Hachette UK Company
www.hachette.co.uk

For my good friend Tony who I've known since the age of 5.
The best drawer and Lego maker.

J.F.

Perhaps the luckiest thing that ever happened to me was
having a great dad (because not everyone gets a good one).
So this book is dedicated to my father, Richard Gough. He
didn't have much of a dad himself, and so he had to work out
how to do it all from scratch. He did an amazing job.
(And in his spare time, he fought a lot of fires, and saved
a lot of lives.) I love you, Dad. Thanks for everything.

J.G.

Rabbit burst into Bear's cave.

"Bear, where do trees go for the Winter?" said Rabbit.

"Trees stay exactly where they are," said Bear, yawning. "You're thinking of birds. Birds fly south for the Winter."

"Well, I think some trees are flying south this year, Bear."

"But trees can't fly," said Bear, "... I think." She tried to reach an early-morning itch, right in the middle of her back. "Ooof ... Can you scratch my itch? It's just there."

"Sure!" Rabbit jumped as high as he could.

"Hmm. That's more of a tickle, Rabbit."

"It's hard to reach the itch, through all your fur ..."

"True," said Bear. "Well, thank you for trying. I will go and scratch myself against my scratching tree." Mmmm ... even the thought made the itch feel less itchy.

"Er, Bear ..." said Rabbit.

But Bear was already walking down to the stream. She looked left. She looked right. "Where—" said Bear.

"That's what I'm trying
to tell you ..." said Rabbit,
catching up.

"Where is my
favourite scratching
tree?"

"Flying south, for the
Winter?" said Rabbit.

Bear looked up into
the sky, just in case.
"No ..."

Then Rabbit
saw something.
He gulped, and
pointed down.

Bear looked.

There, where her scratching tree had been, was a *stump*. Bear bent closer. A stump covered in *tooth marks*.

Giant tooth marks.

Rabbit's knees began to tremble. "Wh … wh … what kind of ferocious Monster could EAT a TREE?"

"I don't know," said Bear. "A hungry one? Which reminds me, let's get some honey, to put on berries, for breakfast."

"WHY AREN'T YOU WORRYING?" shouted Rabbit.

"Because worrying doesn't fix things," said Bear. "But breakfast does."

So Bear and Rabbit went to look for the Honey Bee Tree.

But the Honey Bee
Tree was gone.
The stump was
covered with giant
tooth marks.
"Are you worried
yet?" said Rabbit.

"Hmmm," said Bear.
"Woodpecker lives in a tree …"
"Oh *no*," said Rabbit.
Rabbit ran, and Bear
walked, until they could
see Woodpecker's tree.
"Oh, it's still there!"
said Rabbit. His knees
and elbows stopped
trembling. "Hi,
Woodpecker!"

"Hi! Hi! Hi!" shouted Woodpecker from her nest. "I'll be out in a minute! I'm packing! To Go! Go! Go!"

"Where?" said Bear.

"South! For the Winter! More Parties! More Fun! Fun! Fun! Warmer! HA HA HA!"

"I'll miss you, Woodpecker," said Rabbit. "And your drumming." Rabbit sighed. No more music and dancing in the long evenings ...

Then a loud CRUNCH! came from Very Near By.

15

It sounded like the world's largest rabbit, eating the world's largest carrot.

CRUNCH!

Like a Monster Rabbit, thought Rabbit … eating a Monster Carrot … to give it the energy … to Attack!

This time Rabbit trembled so much, he was worried his ears would fall off.

CRUNCH!

"It's coming from behind that bush!" said Rabbit.

Woodpecker's tree trembled.

"Hey, hey, hey, Bear!" shouted Woodpecker. "Stop shaking my tree!"

"I'm not shaking your tree," said Bear, puzzled.

"Then who is?" said Woodpecker. She stuck her head out to look.

Another **CRUNCH!** came from behind the bush. The loudest **CRUNCH!** yet.

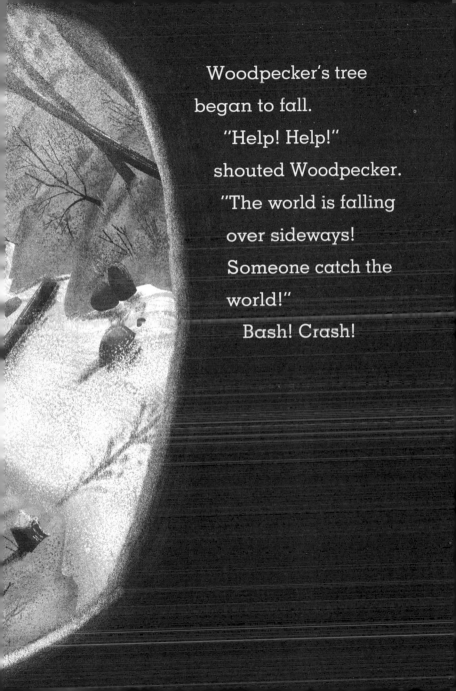

Woodpecker's tree
began to fall.
"Help! Help!"
shouted Woodpecker.
"The world is falling
over sideways!
Someone catch the
world!"
Bash! Crash!

Smash! SPLASH!

The top of the tree landed in the water.

So did Woodpecker.

"Hurgle! Gurgle!" said Woodpecker, with her tail trapped under the tree. "Wurgle! Murgle! SPLURGLE!"

Bear stepped into the water and pulled
Woodpecker free. But ... Pop! Pop! Pop!

"Owwa! Owwa! Owwa!"

"Oh no," said Rabbit.

"Your tail feathers!"

Woodpecker stared

at her bare bum.

"Gone!"

"Can you still fly?" said Bear.

"I'll try!" She tried to fly in a straight line. "Great! I'm flying south! ... No, west! ... No, north! ... No, east! Wwwoooooooooooaaaaaaahhhh!"

She looped the
loop three times,
and crashed into
Bear.

"OOOF," said
Bear. "Oh dear.
Well, your tail
will grow back
by Spring."

"But but but Spring comes after Winter!" said Woodpecker. "That's too late! I'll freeze!"

"Can you make a new nest," said Rabbit, "at the top of a new tree?"

"I can't fly that high, with no tail!"

"Oh dear," said Bear. "So where are you going to live for the Winter?"

"I don't know!" said Woodpecker. "My house is underwater. I don't want to live underwater! Fish pee there!"

"Wait ..." said Bear, and turned to Rabbit. "You didn't live right beside the stream yesterday ..."

"No," said Rabbit, "no, I didn't." "Why did you move your burrow?" said Woodpecker fiercely to Rabbit.

"I didn't move
my burrow!" said
Rabbit. "Someone
moved the stream!"

The water rose even further, and
Woodpecker's house floated away.

"I am very close to being slightly worried,"
said Bear.

"Slightly worried?"
said Rabbit. "SLIGHTLY
WORRIED?! The stream
is climbing the hill! All
the trees are falling over!
IT'S THE END OF THE
WORLD!"

"Oh," said Bear, "I don't think it's that bad."

"Yes yes yes it is!" said Woodpecker. "My house just floated around the bend. I'm going to freeze into an icicle. An icicle with an extra-cold bum!"

"Ah well," said Rabbit, relaxing at last. "At least things absolutely, definitely can't possibly get any worse ..."

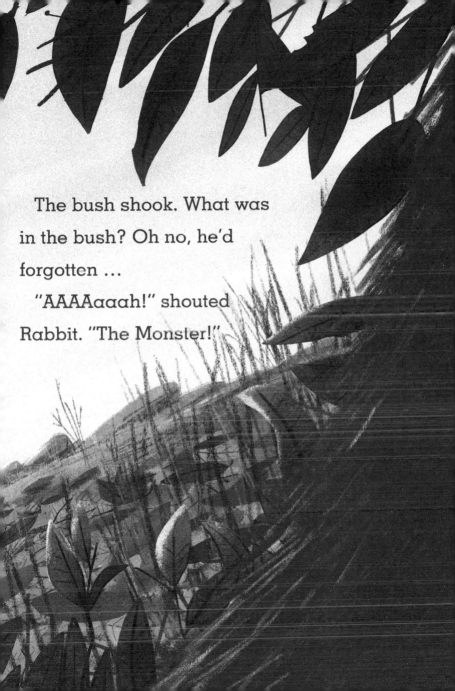

The bush shook. What was
in the bush? Oh no, he'd
forgotten …

"AAAAaaah!" shouted
Rabbit. "The Monster!"

The Monster came out from behind the bush.

"Aaaargh!" said Rabbit. "The Monster's teeth are enormous!"

"Er, yes," said Bear. "True. But the actual Monster is ... quite small."

The Monster walked up to them, reading a piece of bark. It had the biggest two front teeth they had ever seen.

The Monster bumped into Bear's knee.
It looked up.

"Move, silly animal," said the Monster.
"You are standing in the way of
Progress."

"What's Progress?" said Bear.

"Progress is making things ... Newer!"

CRUNCH!

"Bigger!"

CRUNCH!

"Better!"

CRUNCH!

And the creature chewed through a small tree like it was a carrot. Rabbit jumped out of the way as it fell.

"You think this is making things Better?" said Rabbit. "You Monster!"

"I'm not a Monster," said
the creature. "Monsters
don't exist. Only very
silly animals believe in
Monsters."

"OK, OK, OK, if you're
not a Monster," said
Woodpecker, "then WHAT
WHAT WHAT are you?"

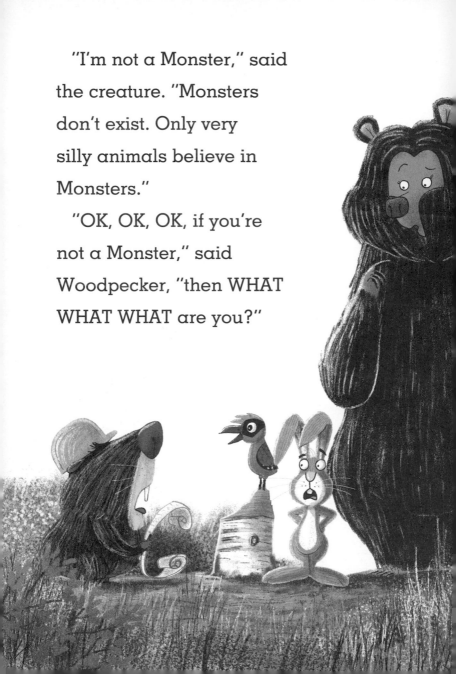

"You can call me ... *Castor Canadensis*,"
said the creature.

"Eh?" said Rabbit.

"It is the scientific name for the North
American Beaver," said Castor Canadensis.

"Why did you move our stream, Castor?" said Woodpecker.

"I didn't move it," said Castor. "I'm just making it Bigger. And therefore Better. Progress!"

"But ..." said Bear, "how do you make a stream bigger?"

"Engineering!" said Castor.

"You put an Engine in our stream?!" said Rabbit.

"No, silly rabbit!" said Castor. "Engineering is the Science of Building Newer, Bigger, Better things." He waved at the deeper, wider stream. "Progress!"

"What has that got to do with our missing trees?" said Bear.

"Everything! Follow me, silly animals, and I'll show you."

They followed Castor around the bend.
Just where their stream normally flowed
into the lake, it was blocked, by a dam
made of trees. Very familiar trees ...

"My scratching tree!" said Bear.

"Our honey tree!" said Rabbit.

"My home!" said Woodpecker.

"Well, it's New," said Bear, looking at the dam. "And Big. But I'm not sure if it's Better. What will it do?"

"Oh, nothing much," said Castor. "Just flood your valley."

"Flood?" said Rabbit.

"Flood?!" said
Woodpecker.
    "How deep?"
said Bear.
    "Oh," said
Castor, "not very
deep." He raised
his hand to slightly
above Rabbit's head.

"Just this high."

Rabbit looked up, horrified. "The stream will come in my back door! AND OVER MY HEAD!"

"Yes," said Castor. "If I do it right."

CRUNCH! CRUNCH! CRUNCH!

CRASH ...

"Well, animals can move house," said Bear. "But what happens to the trees in the valley? Their roots will be underwater."

"Oh, all those trees there will rot," said Castor, stopping work for a moment to point.

"That's terrible!" said Rabbit.

"That's great!" said Bear.

"That's the best best best thing ever!" said Woodpecker. "OK, build your dam!"

"WHAT?" said Rabbit.

"Rotten trees are much much much easier to peck holes in," said Woodpecker. "And rotten trees have lots and LOTS more beetles ..."

"… and beetles' eggs," said Bear, "and honey bee nests and …" It was all too yummy for Bear.

"Ugh!" said Rabbit.
"You dribbled on my
head!"
"Sorry," said Bear.

The water rose higher, and began to drip through Rabbit's back door.

"Castor!" said Rabbit. "This is a disaster!"

"Don't worry," said Castor. "I've done an Important Official Scientific Report. It's full of Good News." He handed the piece of bark to Rabbit. "See?"

ENVIRONMENTAL IMPACT REPORT FOR HYDRO-ENGINEERING PROJECT

BY CASTOR CANADENSIS (SUCCESSFUL BEAVER)

THE SCIENTIFIC FORMULA FOR WATER FLOWING IN A STREAM PAST SOME SILLY ANIMALS IS:

$$\frac{\partial h}{\partial t} + \frac{\partial}{\partial x}\big((H+h)u\big) + \frac{\partial}{\partial y}\big((H+h)v\big) = 0,$$

$$\frac{\partial u}{\partial t} + \frac{\partial u}{\partial x} + v\frac{\partial u}{\partial x} - fv = -g\frac{\partial h}{\partial x} - bu + v\left(\frac{\partial^2 u}{\partial x^2} + \frac{\partial^2 u}{\partial y^2}\right),$$

$$\frac{\partial v}{\partial t} + u\frac{\partial v}{\partial x} + v\frac{\partial v}{\partial y} + fu = -g\frac{\partial h}{\partial y} - bv + v\left(\frac{\partial^2 v}{\partial x^2} + \frac{\partial^2 v}{\partial y^2}\right),$$

$$\frac{\partial Q}{\partial t} + \frac{\partial}{\partial x}\left(\frac{Q^2}{A} + gI_1\right) + gA(S_f - S) - gI_2 = 0,$$

$$\frac{\partial u}{\partial t} + u\frac{\partial u}{\partial x} + v\frac{\partial u}{\partial y} + w\frac{\partial u}{\partial z} = -\frac{\partial p}{\partial x}\frac{1}{\rho} + v\left(\frac{\partial^2 u}{\partial x^2} + \frac{\partial^2 u}{\partial y^2} + \frac{\partial^2 u}{\partial z^2}\right) + f_x,$$

"See what?"
Rabbit stared
at it upside down.

He stared at it sideways.

He put it the right way round
and stood on his own head.
No, it was far too Official and
Scientific for him to understand.
"Tell me in Small, Simple
Words," said Rabbit.

"Sure," said Castor. He looked at the report over Rabbit's shoulder, and turned it back into Small, Simple Words. "A dam will be good news for beavers, fish, snakes, honeybees, tortoises, blue jays, beetles, wolves, frogs, bears, and woodpeckers."

"Huh," said Rabbit. "It can't be good news for EVERYONE."

"No," said Castor. "It's bad news for ... let me see." He turned the page. "Oh yes ..."

BAD NEWS FOR

RABBITS

"AaaAAaaAAaargh!" said Rabbit. "And who else is it bad news for?"

"Oh, just rabbits," said Castor. "But rabbits are usually not very popular, because of their Bad Habits. So the other animals don't mind at all."

Then Mole and Mouse and Vole arrived.

"Hey!" said Mole in his squeaky voice.
"You've flooded my house! I'm angry!"

"Hey!" said Mouse, in her even squeakier
voice. "You've flooded *my* house! I'm
furious!"

"Hey!" squeaked Vole, the youngest and
smallest of all, in a voice so squeaky they
could hardly hear it. She was so angry she

climbed all the way up Castor's fur, to shout in his ear. "You've flooded MY house! And that's MEAN!"

"Oh yes," said Castor, and brushed Vole
off his shoulder like she was an annoying
leaf. "I forgot." He scribbled on his
report. "It's also bad news for moles, and
mice, and voles. But they are Small and
Unimportant and Silly Animals. Well, I'd
better get back to work."

CRUNCH! CRUNCH! CRUNCH!

CRASH ...

"What kind of Monster are you?!" shouted Rabbit.

"Stop calling me a Monster!" said Castor. "I'm a beaver, and beavers are Very Important and Successful Animals."

"Yeah, successful at *ruining people's lives*," said Rabbit. "I don't think he *means* to ruin our lives," said Bear.

Rabbit turned to face Bear and Woodpecker. "You would say that! You're Monsters, too!"

"Us?" said Bear, shocked. "Why?"

"Because you're going to help him flood my home, just to get more honey and delicious beetles' eggs."

"Yes, yes, yes," said Woodpecker, with a sigh. "I guess guess guess we are. But, you know … Delicious beetles' eggs! YUM! YUM! YUM!"

"No," said Bear. "We're not. We are going to help you, Rabbit."

CRUNCH! CRUNCH! ...

"WHAT?" said Castor. He was so surprised, he stopped chewing.

"Help me?" said Rabbit, stunned.

"Listen," said Castor, "if you help that silly rabbit, you won't get all of my lovely delicious rotten trees. And only a STUPID animal would throw away all those tasty beetles' eggs and honey."

Bear shrugged.
"Rabbit is my friend."
"OK, OK, OK," said
Woodpecker. "We'll
both help Rabbit.
He's my friend too."

"But … That's Illogical! Irrational! INCOMPREHENSIBLE!" said Castor.

"Say it in Smaller, Simpler Words!" said Rabbit.

"It doesn't make sense!" said Castor.

"Oh," said Rabbit, and then said, "Oooof …" as Bear and Woodpecker hugged him, and he hugged them back.

"What's happening to your face?" said Castor.

"I'm smiling," said Rabbit.

"What's ... *that*?" asked Castor.

"It's when you're so full to the top with happiness, it floods out."

"Really?" said Castor. "*My* face has never done that."

"You've never smiled?" said Bear. "Then how can you possibly be successful?"

"I am a Success, because ... because beavers work harder than any other animal!" said Castor. "We cut down trees all day, WITH JUST OUR TEETH. Build dams! Build lodges! It's incredibly hard work, and totally exhausting."

"Uh-huh," said Bear. "And what is the Point?"

Castor looked all around him, and up, and down. "The Point of what?" he said cautiously.

"The Point of all this work," said Bear.

"Well ... I work incredibly hard all week, so I can stop work at the weekend."

"OK," said Woodpecker. "So what do you do do do at the weekend?"

"Just ... sort of ... sit."

"With all your friends?" said Bear.

"What are friends?" said Castor.

"Other animals that you like," said Bear.

"And who like you," said Rabbit.

"And that you play with," said
Woodpecker.

"… and talk with," said Mole, "… and
laugh with," said Mouse, "… and dance
with," squeaked Vole, who liked dancing.

"Oh, I don't have any time for that
nonsense," said Castor.
"Dance? By the weekend,
I'm too tired to move."

Rabbit and Woodpecker
stuck their heads into the
unfinished lodge.

"Muddy," said Rabbit.

"Floody," said Woodpecker.

"Hey! Keep out!" said Castor.

"My lodge is just for beavers."

"But there's only ... YOU,"
said Rabbit.

"Well ... yes," said Castor.

"So you work too hard, and you're always tired, and you have no friends," said Bear. "And you sit in the dark, alone, in a muddy, floody hole, all Winter ..." She put an arm around Castor's shoulder. "Poor Castor."

"Stop!" said Castor, putting his paws over his ears. "You're making it sound like I'm not Successful!"

"But you aren't successful," said Rabbit. "Everybody hates you. Your life's a disaster."

"I never thought of it like that before," said Castor. He sat down and started to cry.

Bear frowned at Rabbit. Rabbit shrugged.

Bear said to Castor, "Look, what if we all help you?"

"Help me?"

"Yes, help you to build your lodge."

"But not just for beavers," said Rabbit. "And not so muddy. And floody."

"Bigger?" said Castor. "And better?"

"Yes! We'll build a Club!" said Bear. "For all the animals that don't sleep through the Winter, like Rabbit, or can't fly away, like Woodpecker."

"And we could dance, in the evenings ..." said Rabbit.

"And sleep there, all together, at night ..." said Woodpecker. "Warm! Warm! Warm!"

"Sleepovers!" said Mole and Mouse and Vole, and they hugged each other so hard that all three of them farted.

"You mean ... you want to be my ..."

"Friends!" shouted all the animals, so loud that Owl woke up and joined them.

Castor looked at all their smiling faces. "OK," he said. "I'll try it."

"Good!" said Bear. "OK,
first of all, Rabbit needs to
move above the flood."

Bear and Owl and Castor
and Mole all helped Rabbit
dig a new back door, higher
up the hill.

"I think I'm starting to
understand friendship!"
said Castor.

He was so excited,
he cut down a
REALLY big tree with
his amazing teeth.

CRUNCH!
CRUNCH!
CRUNCH!
CRASH ...

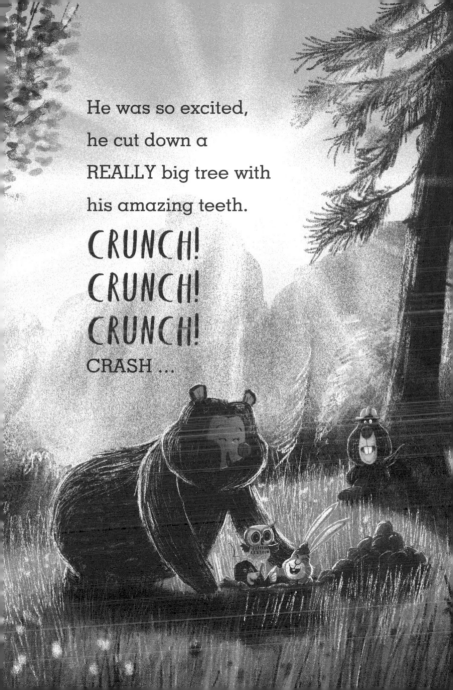

Castor tried to roll it into the stream, but it was too heavy.

"Let me help," said Bear. She pushed too, and the tree rolled.

Splash!

"Ah, that's how helping works!" said Castor. "When a friend helps, it weighs half as much! So it's twice as easy! Mathematics!"

And together, using the special mathematics of friendship, all the animals built the dam. Then they built the lodge. Then they slapped mud on the walls. Then they slapped mud on each other, and had a lovely messy time.

MY LODGE

Inside, the little animals wove a springy, bouncy dance floor out of sticks and twigs. BOING! BOING! BOING!

Even little Vole made beds of crisp dry leaves, for sleeping.

Castor crossed out "MY LODGE" and wrote "OUR CLUB" in neat letters on bark.

They all looked around their brand new Happy Dancing Club and Sleepover Palace.

MY~~LODGE~~ OUR CLUB

"It's New!" said Castor.

"And it's Better!" said Rabbit.

"It's ... Progress!" said Woodpecker.
"Wow! Wow! Wow! Wow! Wow! Wow!
Wow!"

"Zzzz ..." snored Bear. "Hm? Oh! Time for
me to go to sleep for the Winter, I think. So
will you all be OK?"

"Sure!" said Rabbit, and Woodpecker,
and Castor, and Owl, and Mole, and
Mouse, and Vole. "See you in Spring!"

And Bear went back to her cave to
sleep, and had the best dreams ever.
ZzzzZZzzzZzzzz ...

And all the other animals went into their
Dancing Club, and played music and
drummed and laughed and danced.

All except Castor, who just stood back
and watched.

"Want to dance?" said Rabbit to Castor.

"Thank you," said Castor shyly. "But I don't know how."

"I'll show you," said Rabbit.

And Rabbit showed Castor how to dance.

Castor looked around at all his new friends dancing. His face creaked, and began to move. "Something funny is happening to your face," said Rabbit, alarmed. "Are you OK? How do you feel?"

"I feel very, very Successful," Custor said,
and he smiled an enormous smile.

JULIAN GOUGH

© Andreas Riemenschneider 2015

Julian Gough is an award-winning novelist, playwright, poet, musician and scriptwriter.
He was born in London, grew up in Ireland and now lives in Berlin.

Among many other things, Julian wrote the ending to **Minecraft**, the world's most successful computer game for children of all ages.

He likes to drink coffee and steal pigs.

Jim Field is an award-winning illustrator, character designer and animation director.
He grew up in Farnborough, worked in London and now lives in Paris.

His first picture book, **Cats Ahoy!**, written by Peter Bently, won the Booktrust Roald Dahl Funny Prize. He is perhaps best known for drawing frogs on logs in the bestselling **Oi Frog**.

He likes playing the guitar and drinking coffee.

JIM FIELD

© Sandy Foucherand 2016